JELANI'S KEY

Also by D. Amari Jackson
The Savion Sequence

Praise for *Jelani's Key*

"Dramatic, daring, and authentic, Jelani's Key is a page-turning epic chock full of culture, history, and all the things that will enlighten and inspire young readers."

—Kwame Alexander
#1 New York Times Bestselling Author of
The Door of No Return Trilogy,
Writer/Executive Producer, *The Crossover* on Disney+

"Jelani's Key is a coming-of-age story about loving relationships between a boy and his father and grandfather, his newfound friend and their Jegna who takes them on a journey of cultural discovery. It is also a profoundly important story about the intergenerational transference of knowledge and the restoration and preservation of ancestral and cultural history.

D. Amari Jackson has a knack for writing novels with positive male role models of African descent which also includes lessons in math, science, mysteries, and history skillfully interwoven into the narrative. I trust that as young Black boys read Jelani's Key they will aspire to become thoughtful men who appreciate the power of brotherhood, reverence for their ancestors, and understand that they are the inheritors of a cultural legacy they are obligated to preserve and pass on to their descents."

—Anthony T. Browder
Author, and Director of the ASA Restoration Project

"Jelani's Key is a literary and cultural rite of passage for African American middle-graders, both female and male. D. Amari Jackson has managed to carry a real-life phenomenon from ancient Egypt across the endless sands to our urban youth in America using the power of story."

—Stephanie Robinson
Harvard Law Lecturer, Author, and Former Political
Commentator for the Tom Joyner Morning Show

continued

"Poignant, magical, funny, adventurous… Jelani's Key is a story for our times, one celebrating the promise of our children and recognizing just how high, regardless of where they come from, they can fly."

—Charisse Carney-Nunes
Author, Speaker & Education Advocate

"Jelani's Key satisfies the demand for books that make Black boys the hero of the story. D. Amari Jackson is a skilled story-teller whose prose allows the reader to escape into the pages of the book."

—Vanesse Lloyd-Sgambati
Owner, The Literary Cafe Books & Events Bookstore

JELANI'S KEY

D. AMARI JACKSON

jelaniskey.com

AALBC Books for Young Readers
Tampa, FL

Cover art and Design by Justin Jackson:
@BourbenOutKast

Inside design: Natalie Stokes-Peters
(On Point Book Design; www.onpointbookdesign.com)

Paperback: 9780979637438
eBook: 9780979637445
LCCN: 2023941057
AALBC.com LLC
African American Literature Book Club

15310 Amberly Dr, Ste 250
Tampa, FL 33647
(347) 692-2522

Printed in the United States of America
10 9 8 7 6 5 4 3 2 1

DEDICATED TO OUR ANCESTORS...

MAY THEY REMEMBER WHO WE ARE.

CHAPTER 1

TA-TA'S WISH

Ta-Ta was dying. Without the key, all would be lost.

Tears streamed down his mother's cocoa-brown cheeks as she stared into Jelani's watery eyes. Softly, she answered the unspoken question they begged.

"All we can do now is pray for Grandpa, sweetheart."

For the first time in his 11 years, Jelani did not believe what his mother told him. He knew there was something more he could do. After all, last night—just hours after the hospital released his grandfather and told his parents it was "only a matter of time"—Ta-Ta had risen from his wheelchair, entered Jelani's room and told him about the key. As he spoke, the elderly man glowed as if standing by the campfire on their family hiking trips where he'd tell stories of his magical journeys to Egypt.

Since Ta-Ta hadn't walked or talked for years, Jelani knew his late-night visit was a sign his grandfather was getting better. And once he located the key, he knew Ta-Ta would return to walking, traveling and telling stories like he always had.

Sadly, he wouldn't get the chance. The next morning, Jelani father's gently nudged him awake and led him downstairs to the living room. There, he sat on the couch next to his crying mother and little sister, Kara, as his father explained his grandfather no longer lived on earth. He said Ta-Ta had left to "join the ancestors" in a beautiful place where he would no longer feel any pain.

Jelani was stunned. *How was this possible?* Ta-Ta had just spoken to him the night before. As his mother reached for him, he pulled away, ran up to his room and slammed the door. He heard his father's voice telling his mother "it's okay" and to "give him some space." Jelani dived on to his bed and shoved his face into his pillow.

But before the first tear could fall, he felt something odd. Raising his pillow, Jelani saw a small envelope with his name on it. He sat up and pulled a folded note from the envelope as a shiny object tumbled out and disappeared under his bed.

Jelani scrambled to the floor. Behind one of his shoes, something glimmered and he grabbed it. In his hand, shaped like the African symbol Ta-Ta had worn around his neck called an *ankh*, was a golden key!

Jelani gasped and unfolded the note which contained a mysterious poem. Though he was a good reader, he could not understand its full meaning.

> **Beneath the celestial canvas**
> **amidst rich African sands**
> **in the nave of mighty Kemet**
> **near royal burial lands**
> **I remembered my long-lost brother**
> **the temple he lies within**
> **and faced Karakhamun**
> **whose spirit now speaks again**

Next to the strange poem was a short message scribbled in Ta-Ta's handwriting:

Jelani,

Find Karakhamun.

Love Always,

Ta-Ta

Jelani was floored. Though excited he'd located the message and key, he now had more questions than answers. He did know the term *celestial* referred to the starry sky above. Grabbing his dictionary, he found out that *nave* was basically another way of saying 'middle' or 'center' like his own navel or bellybutton in the middle of his body.

But what was the key for? And how was he supposed to *"Find Karakhamun,"* a large African-sounding word he could barely pronounce?

He could ask his dad but Jelani knew his father would be busy the next few days comforting his mom and little sister. And he felt this was too important to wait that long. Jelani also knew that later that evening, just a few blocks away, the special place where Ta-Ta had attended his weekly African history lectures would open.

So after waiting for the sun to drop in the western sky, and with Ta-Ta's key on a chain around his neck, a determined Jelani climbed from his window to the porch below to don his helmet and Egyptian-blue race-bike. He then pedaled up Benning Road to see the one man who could likely tell him about the poem and what the word *Karakhamun* meant.

CHAPTER II

THE BULLY OF BENNING ROAD

Bakare Battle was mean. Make no mistake about it.

Not the kind of kid Jelani, or any of his friends for that matter, wanted to mess with under *any* circumstance. For years, they'd heard horrific tales of the Bully of Benning Road, the man-sized boy who hovered by the door of his broken-down house and chased any boy his age who dared pass by his stoop alone after sundown.

Though few had ever seen him up close since they'd scatter like chickens once his tattered wooden door creaked open, Bakare was known throughout the community as a monster. He was said to be *humun-gous*—big enough to scoop up two screaming kids his age, slam their heads together, and drag them back into his creepy house to never be heard from again.

Then there were the stories from those who claimed to have escaped Bakare's clutches telling of walnut-sized knuckles that could pound the stuffing out of bony little bodies like Jelani's.

Since he lived seven houses down from Bakare, Jelani never had a reason or desire to cross the bully's stoop after sundown. However, this was no ordinary evening. Jelani desperately needed to find out about his grandfather's note and Bakare's stoop was located between him and his destination.

Plus, despite such monstrous stories, there was something about the bully Jelani was not so sure of. Whenever his parents drove past Bakare's house and Jelani gazed from his back seat at its second story window, he could see a large telescope—just like the one Ta-Ta had given him—sitting on a shelf, angled at the sky.

As far as he knew, monsters were not into stargazing.

The idea was to ride as fast as he could past Bakare's stoop so the bully would not have time to react.

That didn't happen. Just before the stoop, Jelani was stunned by how heavy and hard his bike had become to pedal. It felt like an invisible passenger was riding with him, weighing it down, stopping its thin rubber tires from turning.

Jelani looked down and his heart sank. His rear tire was flat. A small nail had punctured its rubber coating.

As he reached for the nail, from the corner of his eye he saw something move. It was as if a massive body was blocking the light of the evening sky, like the *eclipse* his grandfather had once taken him to the West Virginia mountains to see.

Jelani froze. Slowly, he looked up. Standing in front of him was the biggest kid he had ever seen. His body was like one of the linemen Jelani and his dad watched on television during football season. His legs doubled as tree trunks while his arms and hands looked like they could crush a trash can. And his head reminded Jelani of the giant presidential statues at Mt. Rushmore he'd researched online for a recent school assignment.

Trembling, Jelani knew he was about to become the latest victim of the Bully of Benning Road. He closed his eyes and sadly recognized his chances of finding

Karakhamun, whatever that meant, were growing slim.

He was not prepared for what happened next. Instead of receiving the blow he thought would surely come, he heard an unexpected voice.

"Sorry about your grandfather."

Opening his eyes cautiously, a confused Jelani answered slowly.

"You knew my grandfather…?"

The giant boy's eyes dropped toward the ground. He responded softly. "Yeah… he and my dad were friends. They went to Africa together a few years back."

Jelani was stunned. The boy was definitely huge but, surprisingly, he really didn't look that mean. In fact, his saucer-like eyes looked anything but mean… even *sad*. And he had known Ta-Ta.

"I'm Bakare," the large boy continued. "Your grandfather, back when he could talk, told my dad he wanted me to meet you since we both loved to gaze at the stars. But then he got sick before it happened."

"I never knew that," gushed Jelani. "Why didn't you and your dad ever come see us at the house?"

Bakare's eyes dropped toward the ground once more. A pained look spread across his massive face.

"Someone shot my dad… He died a few years back

tryin' to stop some lady from gettin' robbed."

The words cut Jelani like a knife. Several of his schoolmates had lost family members to violence. Each time he heard of someone dying that way, he wanted to cry.

Jelani offered the only words that came to mind. "I'm so sorry, Bakare."

For a moment, the two boys stood in silence under the flickering streetlights. Suddenly, Bakare pointed up at the telescope in his second story window.

"My dad and your grandfather really wanted us to study the stars together."

Jelani shook his head in wonder. "Bakare, I had *no* idea."

"I know," replied Bakare, softly. And just like that, for Jelani, the horrific and legendary tale of the head-smashing Bully of Benning Road disappeared as if it never existed in the first place.

The large boy changed the subject. "Well, wherever you're headed, your ride's not gonna get you there."

Grabbing the bike with one hand, Bakare nodded at Jelani and headed toward the house that now seemed a lot less creepy.

"C'mon man, let's get you fixed up."

CHAPTER III

THE MEMORIAL

It was the first time Jelani had ever seen the photo. Ta-Ta, Bakare's dad and Baba Aton—the man Jelani had come to see—stood smiling in the desert sand in front of a stairway angled downward toward what looked like an underground tomb.

"That was taken in the land they now call Egypt back in 2010," a firm yet kind voice from behind offered. Startled, Jelani and Bakare turned to see a striking figure clad in a flowing African garment. His robe was as colorful as the framed art surrounding him on the center's walls. His eyes appeared to twinkle with wisdom.

11

"Good to see you again Bakare," said Baba Aton, as Bakare rushed to embrace the tall man.

"And if I remember correctly, you are the one and only Jelani."

"Yes Baba," smiled Jelani, returning the man's warm embrace. "It's been a long time since I've been here... wasn't sure you'd remember me."

"Nonsense young African!" scoffed Baba. "How could I ever forget someone as intelligent and remarkable as you?"

Baba suddenly pointed back to the picture as the boys' eyes followed. "I want the two of you to take a good look at this image. You are the living legacy of two great men who transformed my life and our world for the better. As they now walk among the ancestors, it is *you* that carries their proud legacy here on earth."

"This is quite a responsibility," added Baba, with a purposeful nod.

"Yes sir," the boys replied in unison.

Seeing the letter in Jelani's hand, Baba spoke as if he already knew there was a question the young boy wanted to ask.

"So Jelani, tell me exactly what you are searching for."

The memorial was difficult, but amazing. Though he shed tears, Jelani could not believe how many friends and relatives came from so many different places to celebrate Ta-Ta's life. There were endless lines of well-wishers who hugged and kissed him repeatedly. There were cousins, aunts and uncles he had not seen for years who kept talking about how much he'd grown. There were ladies with voices so beautiful that, when they sang, some in the crowd shouted while others cried. There were many who spoke about Ta-Ta's life well before Jelani was born and how he had inspired them.

But of all the wonderful speeches that day, Baba Aton's stood out most. He talked about how Ta-Ta had taken him under his wing as a young man and tutored him in African history. He spoke of how Ta-Ta brought him to Egypt for the first time and helped him establish his touring company. He warmly suggested Ta-Ta was like a father to him and even came close to shedding a tear.

Most of all, Baba Aton fondly recalled the magic and adventure of their many trips together to Africa.

By the time he finished, many in the crowd—including Jelani, his family, Bakare and his mother—were in tears.

At the repast, upon grabbing a plateful of fish, vegetables and plantains, Jelani found Bakare who looked way too big for the suit he was wearing. He nodded at his friend, who also held a plate of food, and the two headed outside into the crisp afternoon to sit by themselves on the hall's front steps. They chewed quietly before Bakare broke the silence.

"That was a beautiful ceremony, man. Think your grandpa would have liked it."

"Me too," agreed Jelani, between bites. "Never knew Ta-Ta and Baba Aton had done so much together."

A familiar voice suddenly sounded from behind.

"There are a lot of things your grandfather wanted you to know Jelani."

The boys quickly put down their plates and scrambled to embrace Baba Aton.

"Didn't mean to interrupt your nourishment, my young warriors," smiled Baba. As they sat back down, his expression suddenly turned serious and he sat down beside them. Jelani thought Baba was going to finally answer his question about Karakhamun.

Instead, he stared deeply into their young eyes and challenged them.

"I have a *very important mission* for the two of you, should you choose to accept it."

CHAPTER IV

THE CHALLENGE

The day had finally come. It was the last morning of winter and an excited but sleepy Jelani jumped up from his covers and ran head first into the wall where the door used to be. Rubbing his eyes, he quickly realized the door had not moved as he scrambled into the bathroom where he fumbled for what he thought was his toothbrush. Grabbing a half-curled tube of toothpaste, Jelani quickly squeezed it on his sister's tiny hairbrush and shoved it into his mouth.

Tasting something hairy, he spit violently before wiping his face, throwing on some clothes and bounding downstairs to the sound of a blaring horn.

"*SLOW DOWN BOY!*" his mother shouted, handing him his coat and a bag with two oranges. "One is for Bakare."

She cradled his head and kissed him before he bounced past his pajama-clad sister watching reruns of *Reading Rainbow* and out the door. Jumping in the back seat, he playfully punched Bakare in the arm, handed him an orange, and avoided his father's gaze in the rearview mirror.

"How is it that Bakare got here first and I live in the same house with you, Jelani?" his father asked, shaking his head.

Jelani waited for his father's eyes to turn back to the road and drive off before grinning mischievously at Bakare.

Sphinx Barbershop was *packed*. All heads in the Benning Road community came out for a cut on Saturday morning and there was a wait even when you arrived early. As they sat listening to D Smoke blaring from pyramid-shaped speakers, Jelani's dad suddenly turned to them and asked, "Do the two of you know what a *Rite of Passage* is?"

"Sir," offered Bakare, "isn't that like going through some sort of test or trial…?"

"That's right Bakare. It's a way of preparing youth for manhood by presenting them with a challenge that will help them learn and grow. Think of what you will be doing tonight at Baba Aton's place as a Rite of Passage. It will just be the two of you. So you're going to have to rely on each other and figure things out to make it through."

Jelani glanced over at the boy who had quickly become his best friend. Bakare nodded back.

His father continued. "Although I cannot tell you what to expect or what Baba has in store for you, I will tell you this." The boys eagerly leaned forward, anticipating the words to come.

"If you come across a challenge that seems too hard to figure out, close your eyes, take a deep breath, and then open them with a new perspective or light."

"You'll often find the answers we seek in life are right in front of us, hidden in plain sight."

The reddening sun continued its downward path as the boys stood in the parking lot of Baba Aton's center on the final day of winter. Baba's instructions were very specific. At Ta-Ta's memorial, after speaking with them on the steps, he had left them with an envelope marked, *The Hero's Journey*, and told them it is what Jelani's grandfather and Bakare's father would have wanted. They had opened it to find a sheet of instructions along with three smaller, sealed envelopes. The outside of the first envelope was labeled *#1 - Open Upon the Last Light of Winter*; the second, *#2 - Open Upon the First Light of Spring*; and the third, *#3 - Open Upon the Climb to the Light of Noon.*

Now, alone in the parking lot, the two examined the instructions once more.

Leave all cell phones, music devices, electronics and food items at home (spring water will be provided onsite). Bring your sleeping bags.

Arrive at the center at 6pm on the evening of the final day of winter. As the sun sets, enter the western entrance of the building and immediately take the stairway down to the basement. Once you pass through the basement door, ALL TALKING STOPS UNTIL YOU HEAR THE RING OF THE MIDNIGHT CHIMES FROM THE CLOCK UPSTAIRS. Basement lights have been disabled. Place your sleeping bags and coats in the closet between the water cooler and bathroom.

Then open Envelope #1. You will still have enough light left from the setting sun to read.

Bakare glanced up at the descending fireball in the sky. "The sun rises in the east and sets in the west so this is the right entrance."

Jelani agreed and the two picked up their sleeping bags, gave each other a pound, and headed into the center.

All was dim and quiet as they headed down the western stairway. They stopped in front of a basement door labeled "DOOR OF AMEN." Next to the words was a strange image of a human with a bird's body.

DOOR OF AMEN

After a deep breath, they opened the door, placed their belongings exactly as Baba instructed, and quietly sat in the middle of the darkening room. There,

Jelani pulled out **Envelope #1** and the two squinted to read by the light of the dying sun on the final day of winter.

> *111 Pushups. You don't have to do them all at once, but you must do them TOGETHER. One cannot finish without the other.*
>
> *When complete, use the words and clues around you to answer the following:*
>
> *"Though the light of your sight will come forth by day*
>
> *its nightly unseen presence still guides your way"*

Question: What am I?

Without talking, a stunned Jelani glanced over at Bakare who closed his eyes and shook his head in disbelief. *111 Pushups? An Unseen Presence?*

And no talking 'til midnight?

As the room grew dark, the boys sat silent, overwhelmed by the challenge in front of them.

CHAPTER V

Into Darkness

The pushups were hard. Their arms throbbed and ached and, between stopping and starting, they had only made it to 39. Though Jelani could barely see his best friend in the dark, he could hear him collapse in exhaustion every time they seemed to get a steady pace going.

Jelani was growing frustrated, but not with Bakare. He recognized how hard, given his massive body, the pushups must be for him. As the two lay on the ground breathing heavily, he wasn't sure how or if they were going to make it through this part of the challenge. And he was worried Bakare might consider quitting and going home.

Then his father's words from the barbershop popped into his head. They reminded him, whenever he felt frustrated, to close his eyes, take a deep breath, and open them with a new perspective.

So he sat up and folded his legs the same way he'd seen his father do when meditating. He closed his eyes and began to breathe deeply. After three breaths, Jelani began to notice how different his breathing sounded from the panting of his exhausted friend. He also noticed the deeper and slower he breathed, the more the energy returned to his body and his mind became clear.

He suddenly had an idea. According to the calculations in his head, they had 72 pushups remaining since 111-39 = 72. Though this was still a lot of pushups, Jelani thought if they paced themselves the right way, they could likely do it. He knew that 12 x 6 also equaled 72, and that set him into motion.

Since they were not allowed to speak, he tugged on his friend's arm until Bakare realized Jelani wanted him to sit up like him. He began breathing slowly and deeply so Bakare could hear it and do the same. Bakare caught on and, for a minute, the two breathed together until the large boy felt much better.

Then Jelani tapped Bakare's arm as if wanting him to do something else. In the darkness, Bakare saw the outline of Jelani's body get into pushup position once more. Though reluctant, Bakare did the same. But this time, when the boys bent their arms on the way down, Jelani inhaled deeply. And when they came back up, he exhaled loudly. Bakare understood immediately and followed his lead.

After six pushups, Jelani tapped Bakare to stop. The two sat up and began breathing together once more for a minute. Then they did six more pushups before repeating their breathing exercise again.

Finally, after 12 cycles of pacing their actions with breathing, the boys collapsed to the floor upon their 111th pushup. Though they could not celebrate their victory with words, a tired Jelani reached over to punch his sweaty friend in the arm.

Hours later, the boys sat glumly in the dark feeling like they had not won anything. It was not yet midnight so they still couldn't talk. It was too dark to see their surroundings or any of the "clues" the envelope had referred to. It was even too dark to read the contents of **Envelop**e **#1** again to make sure they understood what they were supposed to do.

Jelani felt lost as his mind filled with doubt. *Why are we here? Why would Baba leave us alone in the dark without any way of seeing the clues we need to find our way?*

And how was this what Ta-Ta and Bakare's dad wanted for us?

It certainly didn't make things better when he heard a loud snore coming from the large silhouette next to him. Still, he couldn't blame Bakare since they were both tired from the pushups they completed hours before.

Tired or not, Jelani knew they had to figure out their next step. Once again, he closed his eyes and breathed deeply. After three breaths, he opened his eyes and quickly realized something he hadn't before. But before he could react, a loud chime went off from the clock upstairs, signaling the arrival of midnight. The sound scared the sleeping Bakare so much he suddenly exploded to his feet in a wide-eyed daze and shouted, "*MOM!* DID I MISS *BREAKFAST*???"

Jelani collapsed under the weight of his own laughter. He laughed so hard that tears squirted from the corners of his eyes and his sides ached. Once the be-wildered Bakare realized where he was and what he'd done, he began laughing as well.

Bakare's actions were not the only thing that put the boys in a better mood. They had made it to mid-night and could now use their speech to help figure things out. Additionally, Jelani realized the room about them, bit by bit, seemed to be getting *lighter*.

"Bakare, look!" said Jelani. He pointed toward a small corner window near the ceiling beginning to allow a glowing stream of moonlight. Although the stream was too high to give much light to the room below, Jelani saw an opportunity.

"Maybe we can stand on something and put the en-velope up to the light so we can read it again."

Bakare didn't respond at first. Instead, the boy who loved studying the night sky had a different idea. He walked toward the corner window and stood beneath it at a number of different angles. He then turned to Jelani with a confident look.

"Nope my brother. What we're gonna do is let the light come to *us*."

He took another look at the window before walk-ing across the room slowly as if following an invisi-ble downward path from it to the opposite side. Once there, he came face to face with a door to a side room. Opening it fully, the growing light from above was just enough for the boys to see inside. It was a small storage room for books with empty shelves all around it except for four books on a corner shelf at the back.

Bakare began to chuckle. "Of course! Don't you *see* it Jelani?"

Stepping to the middle of the small room, the large boy pointed to the window. "Baba didn't give us any light because he knew, at a certain time, we were gonna have light... *moon*-light! As a bright moon moves in the night sky, light streams to the earth at an angle. And it's about to start beaming through *that* window."

"When it does, I bet you it will shine a light right into the lower corner of this room," continued an animated Bakare. "That's why Baba left these books for us *here* and nowhere else. They likely hold the clues we've been looking for!"

Jelani was stunned both by their discovery and his friend's brilliance. Excitedly, they hugged before grabbing the books off the shelf and placing them on the floor about them.

All they had to do now was wait for the light.

CHAPTER VI

THE UNSEEN PRESENCE

The glowing light was fading. The boys had spent a good amount of time reading from the four books by moonlight and memorizing the contents of **Envelope #1**. Since they could hardly see, it was time to discuss what they had learned.

For hours, they talked about how the books focused on *Kemet*, the native African name for the powerful ancient Egyptian empire. One book showed how the country's long line of Black African pharaohs built the greatest civilization on earth with a higher knowledge of nature, math, science, medicine and spirituality. It revealed that other cultures like Greeks, Romans and Arabs later conquered Kemet when it was weak and, to this day, have tried to hide or erase its great Black African past from history.

Another book covered a special period almost 3000 years ago where Black African pharaohs from the south reclaimed the country from foreign invaders. Known as the *25th Dynasty*, these proud Kushites—with names like *Piye*, *Shabaka* and *Taharqa*—restored Black African rule in the name of their southern ancestors who had ruled Ancient Egypt long before them.

A third book talked about how these ancient Africans studied the motions of the planets and viewed their world in great cycles. It told of how the daily path of the sun and the changing seasons determined their activities on earth. It also noted how Africans created lasting stories to pass down information on life and death, planetary motions, and the cycles of nature.

The fourth book explained how big words can be understood by breaking them down into smaller pieces or *root structures*. It also discussed how some ancient cultures believed letters and numbers were special symbols that could be substituted for one another.

"Okay, I'm gonna say it again and then we'll re-view what we know," said Jelani, as Bakare nodded in the dark.

"*Though the light of your sight will come forth by day, its nightly unseen presence still guides your way…* What am I?"

Bakare chimed in. "Well, from what we've read, we now know the word *Amen* actually means 'hidden' or 'unseen presence.' So we gotta figure out what has an unseen presence at night and why it's important."

Jelani agreed. "Baba has 'Amen' on the basement door as well so it's probably a clue…."

His eyes suddenly popped wide. "*Wait* a minute… The book on ancient Egyptian cycles talked about the word Amen being both the unseen presence of God and a symbol. One of those symbols was the setting sun disappearing below the western horizon each night to become hidden or *unseen*."

"*That's it!*" yelled Bakare. "It's the sun! It fits with the first line, *the light of your sight will come forth by day.* The sun lights our sight and comes forth by day!"

The boys screamed and danced in the dark over their discovery. They had figured out Baba's riddle.

Or had they?

After a moment, Bakare suddenly realized he was the only one still dancing. "Jelani, what's wrong?"

Jelani sighed deeply. "Something's not right… it sorta fits but it doesn't. The first line is fine, but the second says *its nightly unseen presence still guides your way.* I don't see how the sun still guides the way at night…"

"How does it do that?"

The boys grew silent once more.

Apparently, their long, dark night had yet to come to an end.

The resounding chimes from upstairs jarred the boys awake. Neither one of them remembered falling asleep. Though it was still mostly dark, Jelani knew the 6 am chimes meant morning was almost here, bringing with it the first light of spring.

"Come on Bakare. We gotta figure this out so we can move on to the next envelope. The sun's first light will be here soon."

The sleepy Bakare protested. "I don't want the sunlight yet. It's too early. I want the moon… and pancakes with maple…."

The massive boy suddenly sat up straight. "Jelani! The sun… the moon… the light… *It's the sun!*"

Confused, Jelani glanced over at the corner window but saw mostly dark. "Bakare, the sun hasn't woken up yet… and, apparently, you haven't either."

"*No, no* Jelani!" said an excited Bakare. "*Listen* to me. You were right the first time. The answer to the riddle is the *sun*! The sun's nightly unseen presence *does* guide our way. In fact, last night, it guided our way to the clues we needed to answer the riddle!"

Jelani's face remained blank. "What are you talking about? You delirious from hunger?"

Bakare giggled before responding. "No man, I'm good. Just hear me out. The light from the window we read by last night came mostly from the sun. I forgot one of the books mentioned that what we see as moonlight is mostly the light of the sun below the horizon bouncing or *reflecting* off of the moon. So even though we can't see the sun at night, it still guides our way!"

"Of course!" shouted Jelani. "That makes perfect sense! The light of the sun comes forth by day, while its nightly unseen presence still guides our way! *BOO-yah!!!*"

As the darkness peeled away bit by bit, the boys were dancing once more.

CHAPTER VII

Into the Light

As the first light of spring peeked into the basement, the boys were ready. Excitedly, Bakare opened **Envelope #2** and they quickly examined its contents.

> *Take the eastern stairway up to the second level.*
> *Use the sun to unlock your pathway.*
> *222 Sit Ups. You don't have to do them all at once, but you must do them TOGETHER. One cannot finish without the other.*
> *When complete, use the words and clues around you to answer the following:*

A true friend I am
in the middle of the path
I unite with my spirited friend
and climb the stairway
to the Most High

Question: Who am I?

"*222 Sit Ups???*" screamed Bakare. "Oh God, I'll be *pukin' oatmeal* after the first ten."

"Well think of the bright side," replied Jelani. "There's no oatmeal or food anywhere in sight."

Bakare's face dropped. "And *that's* supposed to cheer me up???"

The boys climbed the eastern stairway to the second level where they came to a door labeled "DOOR OF THE KA." Next to the words was an image of two arms reaching up, like a football goalpost.

DOOR OF THE KA

To their surprise, a chain with a six-digit combination lock dangled from the door's handle.

"Wow," offered a stunned Bakare. "Guess there's more work to do to get to the next level, huh?"

Jelani was already deep in thought. He took another look at the contents of Envelope #2 and then nodded his head.

"I don't know the answer yet, but I think I know what Baba is thinking. Just like school, to pass to the next level, you have to apply what you learned at the level before it. So the combination would somehow have to be something we just learned."

He read from the instructions again before stopping abruptly after the first line. A smile slid across his face.

"Use the *sun* to unlock your pathway," repeated Jelani, before stepping up to the lock and twisting it back and forth. Between each turn, he would stop as if calculating something in his head. Bakare watched his friend with curiosity as he reached the sixth twist. To his amazement, Jelani tugged at the lock once and it easily popped open.

"*Huh?*" squinted Bakare in disbelief. "What did you do?"

"Easy," replied a confident Jelani. "The *sun* was the answer to the first riddle and it is also listed here, in plain sight, as a way to 'unlock your pathway.' And remember, one of the books from last night focused on how some ancient cultures believed letters and numbers were symbols that could be substituted for one another… In other words, **A=1**, **B=2**, **C=3**, on and on."

"So all I did was convert the word **S-U-N** to its numeric form of **S=19**, **U=21** and **N=14**. And that turned out to be the right combination, **1-9-2-1-1-4**."

Although thrilled by Jelani's cleverness, the tired, hungry, oversized boy responded without emotion.

"Bruh, I really wanna hug you right now but I'm scared I might make a mistake and eat you."

CHAPTER VIII

THE SPIRIT WITHIN

The sit ups were worse than the pushups. Bakare was toast after 21.

Still, Jelani was on a roll and had an idea. Given his friend was curled up on the floor of the second-level library, he knew the only way they could get through would be to work together. So after getting Bakare to breathe deeply, he sat on the floor facing him and interlocked their feet while grabbing his humongous hands.

"We'll work together as one, like a seesaw,"

explained a determined Jelani. "When you go back, I'll help you up and then you do the same for me."

"Good idea," nodded Bakare. But before they could start, his head tilted like he had discovered something. "*Wait* a minute… You just said we have to *work together as one*. If we do that, then we only have to do *half* the sit ups."

Though Jelani seemed confused, Bakare continued. "Baba's envelope never said we had to do 222 sit ups *each*, it said we had to do 222 sit ups *together*."

"Of course!" shouted Jelani. "That means when we come together like a seesaw, it only amounts to 111 sit ups a piece! And if we can pace them in groups and balance ourselves by helping each other up, then we can get through this a lot easier… *BOO-yah!*"

An hour later, though Bakare lay on the floor moaning, holding his stomach and praying for pancakes, they were done. Now it was time to turn their attention to the second riddle.

Jelani looked it over once more.

A true friend I am

in the middle of the path

I unite with my spirited friend

and climb the stairway

to the Most High

Question: Who am I?

Unlike the night before, there were shelved books in alphabetical order all around them. The only other items in the second-level library were a large mirror covering the back wall and the chiming clock that had awakened them.

Gazing at his own tired image in the mirror, Jelani was unsure where to start. Since they'd been greeted with the word 'ka' on the second-level door next to the image of two arms held upward, he figured it was a clue like the 'amen' on the downstairs door. So he decided to comb the K section for more information on ka.

After some searching, he found a book that discussed the word as a part of the ancient Egyptian cycle of life. It told of how, upon death, a person's *ba,* or soul, would take on the form of a human-headed bird like the image Jelani had seen on the basement door. The ba would come together as one with the ka, the vital force or spirit, to be reenergized, as shown by the two arms reaching upward. It would then fly up to be judged at the highest level, *re*. If it passed judgment at this highest level, it would become free and blessed to live forever.

"So you figure it all out yet man?" joked the voice behind him. Jelani turned to smile at his exhausted but dedicated friend.

"Not yet man, but I just read something that might be important." He told the life cycle story to Bakare who listened with fascination.

"Wow. It almost feels like what your pops said at the barber shop… like the pieces of the puzzle are somehow all there, hidden in plain sight."

For a moment, the boys fell quiet while gazing at their own mirror images and considering these words.

"Pieces," mumbled Jelani, thinking out loud about Bakare's words. "Pieces in front of us, in plain sight… pieces of clues… pieces of… *words*…" His voice suddenly rose. "*ROOT* words! Pieces of words are root words!"

Bakare jumped in recognition. "That makes sense! It would help explain why Baba had us reading about root structures last night… But what does it mean for riddle #2?"

"I don't know," said Jelani, with bent brow. "But I bet you *ka*, *ba* and *re* are likely the root words that form part of the answer... Read it again."

"Okay," said Bakare, standing in front of the mirror. "A true friend I am, in the middle of the path I unite with my spirited friend, and climb the stairway to the Most High... Who am I?"

Jelani moved up to position himself next to Bakare in front of the large mirror. He closed his eyes and began to breathe deeply. Bakare nodded and did the same.

After three deep breaths, Jelani opened his eyes to see Bakare's mouth hanging wide open as if he'd seen a spirit.

"You alright man? You need food?"

"No!" shouted the trembling boy. "I mean, yes, but no... that's not it... Who am I?"

Jelani looked confused. "Well that's the part of the riddle we're trying to figure out..."

"No!" shouted Bakare once more. "Jelani, *who am I*?"

Bewildered, Jelani responded slowly. "You are my best friend... you are..."

Then it hit him.

"You are ***BA – KA – RE!!!***"

42

The boys hugged while whooping loudly. By the time they settled down, all of the pieces of the puzzle had come together.

"You are my *true friend*," acknowledged a smiling Jelani. "In the *middle of the path*—the second level of this three-floor building—I *unite* with you, my *spirited friend*, to answer the riddle. And if we work together to get the right answer like we just did, then we can *climb the stairway* to Level 3, the *Most High*, for the final judgement or test!"

An excited Bakare jumped in. "And there's more! If you look at the spelling of my name, the syllable **KA** actually does lie in the *middle of the path* or second position of the ba and re...   ba - *KA* - re!"

The two were so happy it took the minor chime of the 11am hour to remind them they still had another challenge ahead of them.

And given it would be at the highest level, they knew they would have to rise to the occasion.

CHAPTER IX

FROM THE ROOT

The image on the third-level door actually made sense to Jelani. The book on the ancient Egyptian life cycle had said that if the united ba and ka passed the test at the highest level of re, it would transform into an *akh*, a blessed spirit free to live and soar forever, like a bird.

DOOR OF THE AKH

However, this was little encouragement to Bakare whose brain had shut down upon opening Envelope #3 and seeing a reference to 333 jumping jacks. The large boy sat pouting on the floor of the bare third-level hallway.

"You want more water?' asked a concerned Jelani.

Bakare answered flatly. "Not unless it's waffle-flavored."

Jelani grinned before rereading the contents of the envelope.

> Take the eastern stairway up to the third level. The door will be unlocked.
>
> 333 Jumping Jacks. OR you can add the square root of 110,889 + the square root of 110,889 and do the sum number of jumping jacks.
>
> Complete by the chimes of high noon. Then open the door in the center of the hallway.

"Well the good news is we actually don't know how many jumping jacks we're doing since we have to figure out this equation first," offered Jelani. "If the sum is less than **333**, then that's a good thing. However, whatever we do, we've gotta work fast since we don't have much time before noon."

"Why didn't Baba just say find the square root of **110,889** and multiply times **2**?" asked Bakare. "That would have been easier than telling us to add the same number twice. Moms always tells me to put my math in the quickest and simplest terms."

"That is weird," agreed Jelani. "Maybe it's some sort of clue… but, for now, let's figure out the square root of this humungous number."

Bakare suddenly perked up with a confident smile. "I'm sure you're gonna use this against me, but I'm gonna say it anyway."

"I *eat* square roots for breakfast!"

Upon retrieving paper and pencil from the library downstairs, Bakare detailed his approach. "As you know, a square root of a number like **9** is just a number that can be multiplied by itself to equal **9**. So the square root of **9** is **3** because **3 x 3 = 9**."

"However, it's harder when finding the square root of a large number like **110,889**. But there are ways we can break it down since moms also taught me that math is more about what you *do* know than what you don't. Since 110,889 starts with the number 11, we already know our answer will start with the number 3..."

"Of course!" interrupted Jelani. "Because 4 x 4 is more than 11 so it wouldn't fit."

"Yup," nodded Bakare. "We also know 110,889 is in the *hundred-thousand* group where numbers have five zeros or places. So the square root of such a number would have to be in the hundreds."

"Right," Jelani chimed in. "Because there would be *too many zeros or places* if we tried to multiply say, 3000 x 3000, which equals 9,000,000."

"Exactly!" said Bakare. "So we know our answer should start with a 3 and be in the hundreds range between 300 and 400. Therefore we can ..."

He stopped short as Jelani grinned and shook his head.

"Hidden in plain sight, my brother." Jelani pointed at the 333 jumping jacks. "It's likely the same answer."

Bakare smirked, shaking his head. On paper, he quickly multiplied 333 x 333 to get 110,889.

"Wow." He chuckled. "Baba got us again."

"But wait a minute," said Jelani, turning serious. "Why would Baba have us choose between 333 jumping jacks on one hand, and 333 + 333, or 666, on the other? Of course, we're going to choose 333. Why would he waste the little bit of time we have left putting us on a wild goose chase?"

A troubled Jelani continued as Bakare sat quietly trying to figure out a response.

"I mean, it doesn't make sense... It's almost noon and we can't possibly do over 300 jumping jacks in that amount of time now. I don't mean to sound negative or anything but..."

Bakare suddenly grabbed Jelani. "*Negative...* that's it! Of course, how could I miss that?"

"Square roots are both *positive* and *negative*! Jelani... I'm not doing *any* jumping jacks today and neither are you!"

Realizing Jelani was still lost, Bakare explained. "Let's use the number 9 again. The square root of 9 is, of course, 3 but it is also..."

"*Negative* 3!" shouted Jelani, catching on. "Because -3 x -3 also equals 9!"

Bakare smiled. "And *that's* why Baba set up the equation the way he did. He was testing us to see if we'd do 333 jumping jacks or figure out we *didn't have to*. Since the square root of 110,889 is also -333, we can add the two square roots together to cancel out, or 333 + **-333 = 0!"**

Neither one of them had to guess what to say next.

"BOO-yah!!!"

CHAPTER X

HⒾɢH Nᴏᴏɴ

The high noon chimes were about to strike. Knowing Baba, and considering what they'd been through over the past 18 hours, whatever was behind the door at the center of the hall had to be something special.

Unfortunately for the weary boys, it was locked.

"YOU GOTTA BE KIDDIN ME!" exploded Bakare. "Seriously? After all we've been through? *Who does that?"*

Though Jelani tried to calm him, the hungry boy was on a roll. *"No* Jelani! I will *not* be quiet. This is unacceptable! We followed all of Baba's mysterious rules. We figured out riddles that would have stumped Einstein. We did a *gazillion* pushups in the dark and then, the next morning without breakfast, did *two gazillion* sit ups…"

"What is this, *Dancing with the Stars???* Do I *look* like I belong on that show?"

"And to make things worse, back in the library when you weren't looking, I pulled up my shirt in the mirror and actually *liked* what I saw. That's *not* supposed to happen!"

He continued. "Enough is enough. Baba, if you're out there somewhere listening right now, I apologize, sir, if this comes off as disrespectful. But unless the next stage of this challenge takes place at the Ancient Egyptian Waffle House, *I WANT OUT!!!*"

Finally, Jelani calmed his wide-eyed friend down by getting him to close his eyes and breathe deep. After three breaths together, a sheepish Bakare lowered his head and apologized.

"Hey, I'm sorry I lost it, Bro. It's just that… we've come so far together and worked *so* hard."

"I've never pushed myself this hard before in anything and…" Bakare's voice cracked and trailed off.

Water filled his eyes as he continued. "...and I know that, once we get through this door and complete our final challenge, my dad would have really been proud of me."

Jelani's eyes watered as he stepped to his best friend and placed a hand on his shoulder.

"Bakare, not only could I have not done this without you, I could not imagine doing it with anyone else. Thank you for being my brother when I needed one most. Thank you for being as brilliant and fun as you are. And don't ever apologize for being you."

"And one more thing Bro," said Jelani, with a firm gaze. "I believe—no, scratch that—I *know* that your dad and Ta-Ta are chillin' together at the highest level and smiling upon us right now."

The two boys embraced. As they did, Bakare's large arm brushed the chain around Jelani's neck and something dropped to the floor below. Hearing it, they squinted and stepped apart to look toward their feet.

Ta-Ta's key.

At that moment, loud, singing chimes rang out for the arrival of high noon. Fascinated, the boys gazed at the key, then at the door in front of them, then at each other.

CHAPTER XI

Opening the Door

"Welcome, my young African warriors! You have done well."

Baba Aton stood in the middle of the room dressed in a flowing African robe. The walls around him were adorned with striking images of majestic dark-skinned pharaohs. On a small table in front of him was a large cup and a balance scale with its golden arms supporting weighing pans on each side.

Before the stunned boys could open their mouths, Baba held up his hand to prevent their words.

"High noon is upon us. It is time for you to face your final test. Come."

Jelani placed the chain with the key he'd used to open the door back around his neck as he and Bakare took their places in front of the table. Baba raised the cup and walked over to a large potted plant at the side of the room, holding the cup above it.

"On this special day of new beginnings, we give honor and thanks in the name of our ancestors."

Baba nodded at each boy respectively as he poured water into the soil of the plant and acknowledged the names of their deceased loved ones.

"*Asante* to the spirit of Marcus Jelani Baffour. *Asante* to the spirit of Malcolm Bakare Amankwatia Battle. May they continue to speak through us. *Ase*."

Baba returned the cup to the table before gazing into the boys' wide eyes. "There is but one question remaining to bring our challenge full circle. It is the same question you brought to my *door*. I now return this question back to you."

"What does the word *Karakhamun* mean?"

Jelani and Bakare's faces dropped. They were not expecting Baba to ask them the same thing they'd come to him to find out. After fidgeting for a moment,

Jelani looked over at a nervous Bakare and nodded. His friend nodded back as the two closed their eyes and slowed their breathing.

Jelani replayed the past 18 hours in his head. He thought about the clues, the books and all they had learned. He figured the answer was somewhere within the three levels of knowledge they'd gathered while making their way to this final challenge.

Still, there was another thing for Jelani to consider. There was something odd about the way Baba had said the word *door* that caught his attention. It was almost as if he was giving away another clue.

So Jelani began focusing on the word and its possibilities. *Door… open the door… pass through the door to the next level… three levels of doors at the center… Door of Amen, Door of the Ka, Door of the Akh…*

Something began to feel familiar… *Door of Amen, Door of the Ka, Door of the Akh… open the door to Amen, Ka, Akh…*

Amen, Ka, Akh…

Jelani's eye's suddenly sprang open.

Ka – Akh – Amen…

Karakhamun!

"I got it Baba!" shouted Jelani, breaking Bakare

from his trance. "The words on the doors at each level help make up the word *Karakhamun!* It was right in front of us all along!"

"Yes, Jelani, you are correct," agreed Baba. "But it still doesn't answer the *question*. I'll pose it to you again."

"What does the word Karakhamun *mean*?"

"I'm sorry Baba," said Jelani, shaking his head for answering too early. He turned to Bakare. "Okay, we found that *ka* means vital force or *spirit*."

Bakare chimed in. "And *akh* means that spirit is blessed or, what my dad used to say, *enlightened*."

"And *amen*," continued Jelani, "means the hidden or unseen presence, as in *the unseen presence of the Most High*."

"So if we put it all together… Karakhamun means…"

"…*the spirit enlightened by the unseen presence of the Most High*."

Baba smiled broadly as he held open his arms and the two *young men* rushed to embrace him. After telling them how proud he was of them, he settled them back down while pulling a small box from a shelf at the side of the room.

"Now that you have successfully completed your challenge, I have three gifts I want to give you."

An excited Bakare smiled at Jelani. They had made it.

"And, by the way, Bakare…?"

"Yes Baba?"

"Not one of them is a waffle."

Bakare's face flushed with embarrassment as Jelani doubled over with laughter.

First, Baba handed them a framed picture of Jelani's grandpa, Bakare's dad, and Baba together in Africa at the steps of the Egyptian tomb. It was the same one they'd seen on the wall when they first visited the center together.

Next, he handed them a book he said contained information on the recently discovered tomb in Egypt of a high priest who lived almost 3000 years ago. Baba revealed that the picture with their loved ones had been taken in front of this tomb. The young men gasped when he informed them the tomb was the burial site of an ancient priest named *Karakhamun*.

"Karakhamun was a *real* person?" shouted Bakare, as Jelani's mouth dropped.

"Yes he was," nodded Baba. "And a very special one. Karakhamun, like his name suggests, was a great

spiritual leader in *Kemet* or Ancient Egypt who repre-
sented the pharaoh himself. He was a member of the
royal family who delivered uplifting services and mes-
sages to thousands of people."

"And your loved ones wanted both of you to know
who he was."

Baba smiled before reaching into the box and pulling out an envelope.

It was time for his third and final gift.

CHAPTER XII

FACING KARAKHAMUN

Now they were soaring, up and above cottony clouds through a powder-blue sky streaked with rays of golden sunshine, where two young travelers could place their hopes and dreams as well as their pain. It was a pain forged by the loss of loved ones who had touched and molded their lives yet left them far too soon. It was a pain softened by their current journey to the magical land their loved ones loved most.

When not gazing out the windows of their giant aircraft, Jelani and Bakare had a hard time believing they were actually on their way to Egypt! Neither of them had expected that Baba's third gift was a travel fund set up by him, Ta-Ta, and Bakare's dad years ago for this very occasion. Baba had continued to raise funds after the death of Bakare's dad and Ta-Ta's illness. It was the greatest gift they could ever ask for.

The three of them landed in Cairo, the capital city of Egypt, where Baba took them to go inside the Great Pyramid at Giza. They were stunned by the massive size of the pyramid and wondered how and why their dark ancestors had built something so remarkable.

Afterwards, they took a short ride to the city of Saqqara to see the Step Pyramid built by the famous architect and genius, *Imhotep,* over 4000 years ago. Seeing these extraordinary buildings and learning about the Africans who created them made Jelani and Bakare wonder why their televisions back in America didn't tell them these ancient intellectuals looked like them.

A day later, the three of them boarded a small plane and flew south to Luxor, a city once known by its African name, *Waset.* There, they were amazed as they walked through the massive ruins of the Temple of Karnak or *Ipet-Isut.* Baba explained this beautiful temple was the greatest in the land where Karakhamun and other spiritual leaders would minister to as many as 83,000 people at one time.

Then they visited the Valley of the Kings where a number of pharaohs were buried, including the most well-known, *Tutankhamen*, or King Tut. As they moved from one incredible tomb to another in the blazing hot desert, Jelani teased an awestruck Bakare for not mentioning food even once.

Finally, that afternoon, they rode to a desert site not far from the Valley of Kings that was the home of the tomb of Karakhamun.

"Wow, we're here Jelani," said Bakare, shaking his head in disbelief. "We are actually *here*."

Jelani looked over at his best friend and smiled. Words simply could not express what he was feeling.

The three of them stepped from their vehicle and on to the same land Ta-Ta and Bakare's dad had tread years before. Baba put his arms around their shoulders and smiled.

"Gentlemen! It is time to greet your ancestors."

Together, they walked across the sands before coming upon the stairway entrance where Baba and their loved ones took the photo he had gifted to each of them. Reaching the mouth of the tomb, Jelani stopped and closed his eyes. He thought of his parents and how happy they were to know he was traveling the world. He thought of his late grandfather who had always told him to never let his circumstances or surroundings limit his dreams. He thought about the formerly-monstrous boy up the street who had become a brother to him, one he could count on regardless of the troubles life might bring.

And he thought about his extraordinary ancestor, Karakhamun, who—through Ta-Ta and Baba—had called him to the ground he now stood upon.

Jelani realized that Ta-Ta had known all along. He knew that, as long as we remember and celebrate our ancestors, their spirits will continue to live and speak through us.

For Jelani, finding Karakhamun was finding out about his rich and beautiful African heritage. Finding Karakhamun was finding more about who his grandfather actually was. Finding Karakhamun was finding out that everything has a purpose, and that death is yet another stage in the beautiful and endless cycle of life.

But most of all, finding Karakhamun was about finding himself.

Jelani paused at the top step of the descending stairway. He looked over and nodded at Bakare, who knowingly nodded back. Before entering the ancient tomb, along with taking a picture, there was something else they had to do.

And with the eye-twinkling smiles of two young explorers—and in honor of their priestly ances-tor who'd delivered similarly inspiring words to the African masses thousands of years before—Jelani and Bakare recited their favorite poem as they gazed out beyond the endless sands of Egypt and recognized that no one could ever stop them from soaring.

> *Beneath the celestial canvas*
> *amidst rich African sands*
> *in the nave of mighty Kemet*
> *near royal burial lands*
> *I remembered my long-lost brother*
> *the temple he lies within*
> *and faced Karakhamun*
> *whose spirit now speaks again*

FOR PARENTS, EDUCATORS & OUR FUTURE LEADERS:

Karakhamun Lives! In 2008, the ASA Restoration Project was established by cultural historian and author, Anthony Browder, in honor of the late educational psychologist and historian, Dr. Asa G. Hilliard, III. The project currently funds the excavation and restoration of several 25th dynasty tombs on the West Bank of Luxor, Egypt, including the tomb of Karakhamun. The ASA Restoration Project is proud to be the first and only African American organization to fund excavations in Egypt and conduct primary research on the world's oldest documented civilization.

The ASA Restoration Project is partnered with Dr. Elena Pischikova, director of the South Asasif Conservation Project, who discovered these ancient tombs in 2006. The primary tombs were built 2700 years ago for three Kushite noblemen and priests—Karakhamun, Karabasken and Nesbanebdjed—in an area near the Valley of the Kings.

Karakhamun was a priest of Amun at Karnak Temple, the largest temple ever constructed. He is believed to be the son of Shabaka, the second king of the 25th dynasty. Karnak Temple is said to have housed over 83,000 priest and priestesses and is the largest temple complex in the world.

Karabasken was the mayor of Waset (Luxor), the political and religious capital of ancient Egypt. Waset is the home of Karnak Temple and Luxor Temple, which are 1.7 miles apart and connected by a 250-foot-wide avenue lined with 1350 sphinxes.

Karakhamun's burial chamber is 60 feet underground and is accessed via a large shaft. Its walls are beautifully adorned with painted images of the "weighing of the soul" and the 42 judges of the deceased. The ceiling is painted with a wonderful image of Nut, the goddess who represents the Milky Way.

The opening of the site is planned for the fall of 2025. In honor of the planned 2025 opening, 25% of the proceeds of *Jelani's Key* will go to the ASA Restoration Project, the non-profit tax-exempt organization funding the restoration of Karakhamun's Temple Tomb.

For more information or to donate to the ASA Restoration Project, go to ikg-info.com

Aerial recreation of ASA Restoration Project on the West Bank of Luxor, Egypt

ASA Restoration Project director Anthony Browder in Karakhamun's tomb with daughter Atlantis

Browder poses next to the sculpted
image of Karakhamun

Karakhamun Burial Chamber Steps

Ꭺᴜᴛʜᴏʀ Ɲᴏᴛᴇ & Ɓɪᴏ

Amari in Egypt in 2010

Asante to Justin, Imani, Alaia and Kaleb for inspiring, Sis for reviewing, Dad for believing, Mom for rallying the ancestors, Nova for her remaining spirit, Candace for helping to visualize the characters of Jelani and Bakare, Troy for championing Black books, and Baba Tony for mentoring, energizing, and introducing me to Karakhamun on that magical fall day in 2010 as we traversed the land of our ancestors.

D. AMARI JACKSON is a creator, TV/web/film producer, ghost writer, songwriter, and award-winning journalist. He is author of the 2011 novel *The Savion Sequence*; creator/writer/coproducer of the 2012-2014 web series *The Book Look*; writer/coproducer of the 2016 film *Edge of the Pier*; writer of the upcoming documentary *Global Assignment: The Life and Times of Dr. Runoko Rashidi*; and Senior Writer for BlackArtinAmerica.com. A father, grandfather, and longtime martial artist, Amari lives in the Atlanta area.

Learn more at JelanisKey.com